DATE DUE

NOV 2 8			
FEB 2 7 1986			
DEC 1 4 1992			
APR 2 2 1994			

**First published in the United States 1988
by Chronicle Books**

Text copyright © 1987 by Ulf Nilsson
Illustrations copyright © 1987 by Eva Eriksson
All rights reserved. No part of this book may
be reproduced in any form without written
permission from the publisher.
First published in Sweden 1987 by Bonniers
Printed in Denmark
Library of Congress
Cataloging-in-Publication Data

Nilsson, Ulf, 1948-
    Little Bunny & Her friends.
    Translation of: Lilla syster Kanin och alla
hennes vänner.
    Summary: Six animal friends have a
problem finding a recreational activity that
they will all be able to complete and enjoy.
    [1. Animals–Fiction. 2. Play–Fiction]
I. Eriksson, Eva. II. Title.
PZ7.N589Lj 1988   [E]   88-2853
ISBN 0-87701-526-0

Distributed in Canada by
Raincoast Books
112 East Third Avenue
Vancouver, B.C.
V5T 1C8

10 9 8 7 6 5 4 3 2 1

Chronicle Books
San Francisco, California

Little Bunny & Her Friends

Ulf Nilsson ❦ Eva Eriksson

Chronicle Books
San Francisco

One afternoon, Little Bunny and her friends
gathered together to play.

"Let's hop up and down," said Little Bunny.

But the others wouldn't.

"No, let's splash in the pond," suggested Frog.

But the others couldn't.

"Let's roll in the mud," squealed Pig.

But the others wouldn't.

"Let's fly in the sky," squawked Crow.

But the others couldn't.

"Wait a minute," squeaked Mouse.
"We need something we can all do together."

And with that, she scampered into a tiny mouse-hole.

Little Bunny tried to scamper in after her, but she got stuck.

"Let's race through the meadow," buzzed Bumblebee.

Big Brother Rabbit arrived with his book just as
Bumblebee took off into the air.

The others chased after Bumblebee,

but poor Snail couldn't.

"Let's slither up a tree," he suggested.

But Frog thought that was a terrible idea.

"There must be *something* we can all do together," sighed Little Bunny.

So she thought and she thought and she thought.
Then she had an idea.

And together all the friends had a wonderful time.